T0078044

Friend
Bird

Alone can be lonely, be open to those who ask you to join in

Inspired by a children's book
FRIEND BIRD by
Tim G. Wiley 1987
1st Edition

Elizabeth Wiley MA JD, Pomo Elder

Order this book online at www.trafford.com
or email orders@trafford.com

Most Trafford titles are also available at major online book retailers.

Print information available on the last page.

ISBN: 978-1-6987-0713-6 (sc)
ISBN: 978-1-6987-0714-3 (e)

Trafford rev. 11/11/2021

Trafford
PUBLISHING® www.trafford.com
North America & international
toll-free: 844-688-6899 (USA & Canada)
fax: 812 355 4082

INTRODUCTION

Friend Bird

A book written by a young teen with cancer to raise money for another teen

It was the day after Christmas vacation, my sons returned to school.

My older son came home and said the school nurse had said he had to see his doctor and get a medical clearance before coming back to school. He called and went straight in to see the doctor, he came back and said Mom, he wants to see you, meet him at the hospital.

When we arrived at the hospital my son went with a nurse to be prepared for admission in an isolation room to protect him from anything that could worsen his condition.

The doctor told me what the nurse had said, and what he had seen, what the primary tests were bringing back. It was a bone and blood cancer that was considered terminal.

From a happy, lucky, top student, who based on testing had received application invitations from several top colleges, universities and even from the Air Force Academy that he had sent preliminary requests for admission to attend.......he was dying.

From the lead singer in a punk band, working on his Eagle Scout final projects, a popular member of the community........he was dying.

The doctor waited for some tests and then said he would tell him.

I said, no, I will tell him.

I said, all that Native American religious healing learning, and Catholic school religious training, the Jewish classes to Bar Mitzvah his Godfather (Jewish) and Boy Scouts it was time to dig in and get courage and faith.

He was diagnosed with a very rare strain of aplastic anemia, and being sent to the prestigious City of Hope in one day. We knew it was bad. Our doctor told us that one of the two research doctors in the whole world on this type of bone and blood cancer had just come to City of Hope a couple of weeks before.

We waited while my son was admitted to the pediatric cancer ward. A woman approached me and introduced herself as the Mom of a 14 year old who had relapsed for the third time. There was nothing anyone in the world could find to do medically to save her. We all prayed. The Mom told me that we are the lucky ones, because we now knew how precious the minutes with our children were. How many times she asked, had we heard other parents saying they could hardly wait for their child to graduate, be eighteen and leave.

How many parents saw school as a reprieve from parenthood, and camp, and visits to grandparents were also a light at the end of the tunnel vision of getting those kids to 18 and out the door. We were blessed to know those few moments of this precious gift meant a lot more than an expensive punishment for our brief desire for sex, or the baby magazine idea of having a child. How many children were abandoned in foster care, or not able to be managed turned over to juvenile in house probation programs.

My younger son was devastated. They attempted to match bone marrow, but their bone marrow did not match, nor did mine......nor the bone marrow of my sister that was old enough to be considered for a transplant. The doctor then decided because of the kind of aplastic anemia my son had, a transplant would probably not work anyway.

The doctor told my son, who was in isolation, no visitors except his brother and myself, and both of us had to wear complete protective gear from head to toe. Then the doctor told him that he apologized, but this was time to grow up, sixteen, he had to man up and make a choice, to not get treatment and die within weeks, in isolation in a hospital, OR attempt a newly developed research project which quite honestly could kill him unless it worked.

We told my son, this is your choice. DO not live for us, you have to make your own choice. Of course we want you to live, but this is about you, not us. He was too old for us to make the choice for him.

After he left 41 days in isolation at the hospital, he was sent home to spend more days in isolation. We had to clean his room out, we moved him to a room near to our second bathroom, and cleaned everything, everyday with special cleaners to make sure he was safe from infections as the treatments had left his immune system low. When he was allowed to return to school many of the teens had no idea what his disease was, and were afraid. Many teens are just afraid of disease, and do not understand that cancer is NOT able to be caught like a cold.

He was NO LONGER allowed to many of his previous activities because a simple bruise could cause his thinned blood to start bleeding inside his body and cause him to bleed all his blood. Many of his previous friends did not understand this.

Then he hears that another teen, from another country, had the same type of cancer, but could not get treatment because at that time grants were so restricted, only Americans could be in the research programs. SO, he decided as his Eagle project for Scouting to write a book, and use it to raise money for that other teen to get treatment where he had.

He contacted many corporations and one said, if you get the book published, we will publish it in our format and make it available at schools all over the country to educate children about other children with severe illness and terminal illness.

Another Corporation said, if you get the book published, and the little toy that goes with it (a friend bird of course) we will make our own small copies of the book, and toy to give to children who come to our restaurants all over the country.

He found a group that helped terminally ill children get their last wishes and dreams come true.

He found a celebrity that said, YES, I will help, I too will give the toys and books to kids in my programs, and put a coupon on my labels so people can donate to help other kids with the problem of not living in the areas for grants to help them.

Then he turned 18. OH, sad said the Foundation, we can not help any teen once they turn 18. it is in our grants. The book and toys were never published or copyrights, patented or made. It made him and his brother very sad, and very bitter. BUT, they spent time writing to people to change the grants so that a child, or teen once started could get the help they had been promised.

Over the years, it has taken both of my sons a lot of support and help to stop thinking being bitter and feel alone. To remind themselves of all the people who DID help, especially the doctor who found the research project to help my son, and the research doctor who gave his own blood at one time to help. To remember the people from our unions, churches, community groups, and schools that donated blood for my son. We were told it was the most blood ever donated at that time for one person......he had only needed one pint after all, we believe that was from prayer from all over the country. THIS book is inspired by the book he wrote, which will be published later this year, and hopefully helps us all remember to BE Friend birds, not just need one.....both are OK places to be. God bless.

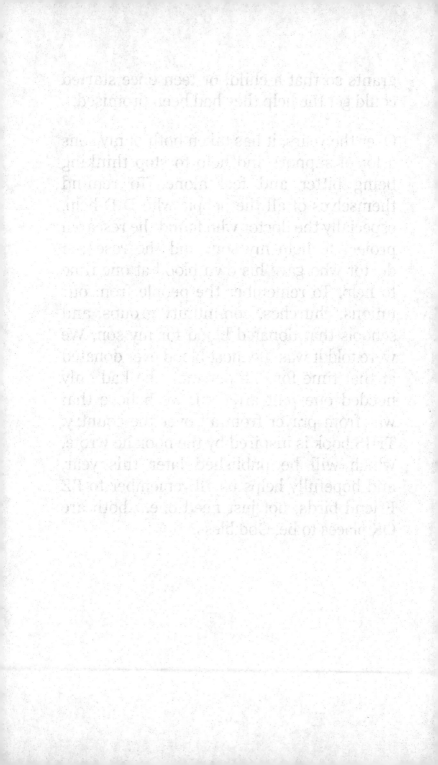

FRIEND BIRD

....

A lonely little bird

Friend bird was a cute little bird, he was fun, he thought, but he had NO friends.

Are YOU a cute little person? Draw yourself here.

Do you have friends? Draw a picture of your friends.

FRIEND BIRD PLAYS AT SCHOOL, BULLIES TELL HIM TO GO AWAY, AT LUNCH, AT RECESS........

Are there bullies at your school? In your neighborhood, at day care? Draw them.

DO YOU bully anyone? Talk about it. Draw a picture of yourself being a bully?

Friend Bird would watch the others play, but he was not allowed to play.

The other birds said "we do not want you to play, you are no good".

Friend bird tried not to cry, would run home and cry alone in his room.

Draw a picture of yourself crying alone.

One day Friend Bird met another bird, that bird DID talk to him. She found him crying behind a tree.

"Why are you crying" said New Bird? New Bird gave Friend Bird a paper napkin to wipe his nose.

Friend Bird told New Bird about the birds who would not let him play with them. She listened quietly.

If someone is sad, can you listen quietly? Draw a picture of you listening quietly. Can you sit and listen without making the person feel like a victim? or ignored?

What does helping a person feel like a victim instead of a loved friend look like?

What does looking like listening, but really not look like? How can you change?

New Friend said "let's go play". "what do you like to do to laugh and have fun?"

If you are feeling sad and alone, what do YOU do to feel happier who do you invite to share FUN, not just the anger, or sadness? Draw a picture of YOU feeling sad and bitter.

*Who do you go to to help you feel better?
Draw a picture of the Friends in your life,
it might be your Grandparents, a neighbor,
your teacher, your parents, it does not have
to be a person you "wish" would make you
feel better.*

Friend Bird and New Friend start to play in the park, laughing and shouting, having fun, they have forgotten about the others. The others begin to look and see what all the fun is about.

Draw a picture of you having fun with, or without a friend to help you feel happy and filled with joy.

Soon the other birds come over and one by one ask if they can join the fun. Friend Bird and New Friend say YES. All the birds begin to have so much fun that others join in.

During a break, when they are all sitting on the lawn, New Bird says, this is so much fun, lets do this all the time. The other birds say YES. BUT, says New Bird, we have to promise that we will not bully or leave each other out again. The other birds and new friends all smile and nod.

Sometimes a good person is a Grandparent, or parent, or teacher: draw a picture of you having fun reading a book, or playing a board game with someone, having so much fun the others will come over and want to play.

Draw a picture of you finding someone who is not allowed to play with the others either.

CLOSING AND OTHER BOOKS BY AUTHOR AND TEAM

. . . .

Closing:

This book is one of many that we use, as workbooks, or to read and discuss in groups of youth and parents, as well as to train teachers, counselors, pastors, and other religious leaders as well as principals and superintendents of education programs to make each child a well respected part of their whole program.

We hope that parents of disabled, or severely ill children and teens will take this book, and the original book "FRIEND BIRD" to facilitate for everyone to give and receive love and support.

We hope that everyone will learn to be more supportive to those who have any type of disability. Mental illness, addictions of every kind (including gossiping, and criticizing others to make oneself feel OK) and physical disabilities are hard to bear, but all those with these problems need to learn about the rights of others as well. If a person wants to be part of a happy group, they have to do their part. Maybe seeing a doctor, or specialist, or going into a treatment program is what they need to do to help themselves be the person who CAN enjoy life and support the problems of the others when needed instead of only thinking of themselves and their problems.

Books and workbooks in our programs:

All of our group of books, and workbooks contain some work pages, and/or suggestions for the reader, and those teaching these books to make notes, to go to computer, and libraries and ask others for information to help these projects work their best.

To utilize these to their fullest, make sure YOU model the increased thoughts and availability of more knowledge to anyone you share these books and workbooks with in classes, or community groups.

Magazines are, as noted in most of the books, a wonderful place to look for and find ongoing research and information. Online search engines often bring up new research in the areas, and newly published material.

We all have examples of how we learned and who it was that taught us.

One of the strangest lessons I have learned was walking to a shoot in downtown Los Angeles. The person who kindly told me to park my truck in Pasadena, and take the train had been unaware that the weekend busses did NOT run early in the morning when the crews had to be in to set up. That person, being just a participant, was going much later in the day, taking a taxi, and had no idea how often crews do NOT carry purses with credit cards, large amounts of cash, and have nowhere to carry those items, because the crew works hard, and fast during a set up and tear down and after the shoot are TIRED and not looking to have to find items that have been left around, or stolen.

As I walked, I had to travel through an area of Los Angeles that had become truly run down and many homeless were encamped about and sleeping on the sidewalks and in alleys. I saw a man, that having worked in an ER for many years I realized was DEAD. I used to have thoughts about people who did not notice people needing help, I thought, this poor man, this is probably the most peace he has had in a long time. I prayed for him and went off to my unwanted walk across town. As I walked, I thought about myself, was I just heartless, or was I truly thinking this was the only moment of peace this man had had for a long time and just leaving him to it. What good were upset neighbors, and police, fire trucks and ambulances going to do. He was calmly, eyes open, staring out at a world that had failed him while alive, why rush to disturb him now that nothing could be done.

I did make sure he was DEAD. He was, quite cold rigid.

I learned that day that it is best to do what a person needs, NOT what we need.

Learning is about introspection and grounding of material. Passing little tests on short term memory skills and not knowing what it all means is NOT education, or teaching.

As a high school student, in accelerated Math and Science programs, in which I received 4.0 grades consistently, I walked across a field, diagonally, and suddenly all that math and science made sense, it was not just exercises on paper I could throw answers back on paper, but I realized had NO clue as to what it all really meant.

OTHER BOOKS BY
THIS AUTHOR, AND TEAM

Most, if not all, of these books are written at a fourth grade level. FIrst, the author is severely brain damaged from a high fever disease caused by a sample that came in the mail, without a warning that it had killed during test marketing. During the law suit, it was discovered that the corporation had known prior to mailing out ten million samples, WITHOUT warnings of disease and known deaths, and then NOT telling anyone after a large number of deaths around the world started. Second, the target audience is high risk youth, and young veterans, most with a poor education before signing into, or being drafted into the military as a hope Many of our veterans are Vietnam or WWII era.

Maybe those recruiting promises would come true. They would be trained, educated, and given chance for a home, and to protect our country and its principles. Watch the movies Platoon, and Born on the Fourth of July as well as the Oliver Stone series on history to find out how these dreams were meet.

DO NOT bother to write and tell us of grammar or spelling errors. We often wrote these books and workbooks fast for copyrights. We had learned our lessons about giving our material away when one huge charity asked us for our material, promising a grant, Instead, we heard a couple of years later they had built their own VERY similar project, except theirs charged for services, ours were FREE, and theirs was just for a small group, ours was training veterans and others to spread the programs as fast as they could. They got a Nobel Peace prize. We keep saying we are not bitter, we keep saying we did not do our work to get awards, or thousands of dollars of grants....but, it hurts. Especially when lied to and that group STILL sends people to US for help when they can not meet the needs, or the veterans and family can not afford their "charitable" services. One other group had the nerve to send us a Cease and Desist using our own name. We said go ahead and sue, we have proof of legal use of this name for decades. That man had the conscience to apologize, his program was not even FOR veterans or first responders, or their families, nor high risk kids. But we learned. Sometimes life is very unfair.

We got sued again later for the same issue. We settled out of Court as our programs were just restarting and one of the veterans said, let's just change that part of the name and keep on training veterans to run their own programs. Smart young man.

Book List:

DRAGON KITES and other stories:

The Grandparents Story list will add 12 new titles this year. We encourage every family to write their own historic stories. That strange old Aunt who when you listen to her stories left a rich and well regulated life in the Eastern New York coastal fashionable families to learn Telegraph messaging and go out to the old west to LIVE her life. That old Grandfather or Grandmother who was sent by family in other countries torn by war to pick up those "dollars in the streets" as noted in the book of that title.

Books in publication, or out by summer 2021

Carousel Horse: A Children's book about equine therapy and what schools MIGHT be and are in special private programs.

Carousel Horse: A smaller version of the original Carousel Horse, both contain the workbooks and the screenplays used for on site stable programs as well as lock down programs where the children and teens are not able to go out to the stables.

Spirit Horse II: This is the work book for training veterans and others interested in starting their own Equine Therapy based programs. To be used as primary education sites, or for supplementing public or private school programs. One major goal of this book is to copyright our founding material, as we gave it away freely to those who said they wanted to help us get grants. They did not. Instead they built their own programs, with grant money, and with donations in small, beautiful stables and won....a Nobel Peace Prize for programs we invented. We learned our lessons, although we do not do our work for awards, or grants, we DO not like to be ripped off, so now we copyright.

Reassessing and Restructuring Public Agencies; This book is an over view of our government systems and how they were expected to be utilized for public betterment. This is a Fourth Grade level condemnation of a PhD dissertation that was not accepted be because the mentor thought it was "against government". The first paragraph noted that a request had been made, and referrals given by the then White House.

Reassessing and Restructuring Public Agencies; TWO. This book is a suggestive and creative work to give THE PEOPLE the idea of taking back their government and making the money spent and the agencies running SERVE the PEOPLE ;not politicians. This is NOT against government, it is about the DUTY of the PEOPLE to oversee and control government before it overcomes us.

Could This Be Magic? A Very Short Book. This is a very short book of pictures and the author's personal experiences as the Hall of Fame band VAN HALEN practiced in her garage. The pictures are taken by the author, and her then five year old son. People wanted copies of the pictures, and permission was given to publish them to raise money for treatment and long term Veteran homes.

Carousel TWO: Equine therapy for Veterans. publication pending 2021

Carousel THREE: Still Spinning: Special Equine therapy for women veterans and single mothers. This book includes TWELVE STEPS BACK FROM BETRAYAL for soldiers who have been sexually assaulted in the active duty military and help from each other to heal, no matter how horrible the situation. publication pending 2021

LEGAL ETHICS: AN OXYMORON. A book to give to lawyers and judges you feel have not gotten the justice of American Constitution based law (Politicians are great persons to gift with this book). Publication late 2021

PARENTS CAN LIVE and raise great kids.

Included in this book are excerpts from our workbooks from KIDS ANONYMOUS and KIDS JR, and A PARENTS PLAIN RAP (to teach sexuality and relationships to their children. This program came from a copyrighted project thirty years ago, which has been networked into our other programs. This is our training work book. We asked AA what we had to do to become a real Twelve Step program as this is considered a quasi twelve step program children and teens can use to heal BEFORE becoming involved in drugs, sexual addiction, sexual trafficking and relationship woes, as well as unwanted, neglected and abused or having children murdered by parents not able to deal with the reality of parenting. Many of our original students were children of abuse and neglect, no matter how wealthy. Often the neglect was by society itself when children lost parents to illness, accidents or addiction. We were told, send us a copy and make sure you call it quasi. The Teens in the first programs when surveyed for the outcome research reports said, WE NEEDED THIS EARLIER. SO they helped younger children invent KIDS JR. Will be republished in 2021 as a documentary of the work and success of these projects.

Addicted To Dick. This is a quasi Twelve Step program for women in domestic violence programs mandated by Courts due to repeated incidents and danger, or actual injury or death of their children.

Addicted to Dick 2018 This book is a specially requested workbook for women in custody, or out on probation for abuse to their children, either by themselves or their sexual partners or spouses. The estimated national number for children at risk at the time of request was three million across the nation. During Covid it is estimated that number has risen. Homelessness and undocumented families that are unlikely to be reported or found are creating discussion of a much larger number of children maimed or killed in these domestic violence crimes. THE most important point in this book is to force every local school district to train teachers, and all staff to recognize children at risk, and to report their family for HELP, not punishment. The second most important part is to teach every child on American soil to know to ask for help, no matter that parents, or other relatives or known adults, or unknown adults have threatened to kill them for "telling". Most, if not all paramedics, emergency rooms, and police and fire stations are trained to protect the children and teens, and get help for the family. PUNISHMENT is not the goal, eliminating childhood abuse and injury or death at the hands of family is the goal of all these projects. In some areas JUDGES of child and family courts were taking training and teaching programs themselves to HELP. FREE.

Addicted to Locker Room BS. This book is about MEN who are addicted to the lies told in locker rooms and bars. During volunteer work at just one of several huge juvenile lock downs, where juveniles who have been convicted as adults, but are waiting for their 18th birthday to be sent to adult prisons, we noticed that the young boys and teens had "big" ideas of themselves, learned in locker rooms and back alleys. Hundreds of these young boys would march, monotonously around the enclosures, their lives over. often facing long term adult prison sentences.

The girls, we noticed that the girls, for the most part were smart, had done well in school, then "something" happened. During the years involved in this volunteer work I saw only ONE young girl who was so mentally ill I felt she was not reachable, and should be in a locked down mental health facility for help; if at all possible, and if teachers, and others had been properly trained, helped BEFORE she gotten to that place, lost in the horror and broken of her childhood and early teen years.

We noticed that many of the young women in non military sexual assault healing programs were "betrayed" in many ways, by step fathers, boyfriends, even fathers, and mothers by either molestation by family members, or allowing family members or friends of parents to molest these young women, often as small children. We asked military sexually assaulted young women to begin to volunteer to help in the programs to heal the young girls and teens, it helped heal them all.

There was NOTHING for the boys that even began to reach them until our research began on the locker room BS theory of life destruction and possible salvaging by the boys themselves, and men in prisons who helped put together something they thought they MIGHT have heard before they ended up in prison.

Americans CAN Live Happily Ever After. Parents edition. One Americans CAN Live Happily Ever After. Children's edition Two.

Americans CAN Live Happily Ever After. Three. After Covid. This book includes "Welcome to America" a requested consult workbook for children and youth finding themselves in cages, auditoriums on cots, or in foster group homes or foster care of relatives or non-relatives with NO guidelines for their particular issues. WE ASKED the kids, and they helped us write this fourth grade level workbook portion of this book to help one another and each other. Written in a hurry! We were asked to use our expertise in other youth programs, and our years of experience teaching and working in high risk youth programs to find something to help.

REZ CHEESE Written by a Native American /WASP mix woman. Using food, and thoughts on not getting THE DIABETES, stories are included of a childhood between two worlds.

REZ CHEESE TWO A continuation of the stress on THE DIABETES needing treatment and health care from birth as well as recipes, and stories from Native America, including thoughts on asking youth to help stop the overwhelming numbers of suicide by our people.

BIG LIZ: LEADER OF THE GANG Stories of unique Racial Tension and Gang Abatement projects created when gangs and racial problems began to make schools unsafe for our children.

DOLLARS IN THE STREETS, ghost edited for author Lydia Caceras, the first woman horse trainer at Belmont Park.

95 YEARS of TEACHING:

A book on teaching, as opposed to kid flipping

Two teachers who have created and implemented systems for private and public education a combined 95 plus years of teaching talk about experiences and realities and how parents can get involved in education for their children. Included are excerpts from our KIDS ANONYMOUS and KIDS JR workbooks of over 30 years of free youth programs.

A HORSE IS NOT A BICYCLE. A book about pet ownership and how to prepare your children for responsible pet ownership and along the way to be responsible parents. NO ONE needs to own a pet, or have a child, but if they make that choice, the animal, or child deserves a solid, caring forever home.

OLD MAN THINGS and MARE'S TALES. this is a fun book about old horse trainers I met along the way. My husband used to call the old man stories "old man things", which are those enchanting and often very effective methods of horse, pet, and even child rearing. I always said I brought up my children and my students the same as I had trained horses and dogs......I meant that horses and dogs had taught me a lot of sensible, humane ways to bring up an individual, caring, and dream realizing adult who was HAPPY and loved.

STOP TALKING, DO IT

ALL of us have dreams, intentions, make promises. This book is a workbook from one of our programs to help a person make their dreams come true, to build their intentions into goals, and realities, and to keep their promises. One story from this book, that inspired the concept is a high school kid, now in his sixties, that was in a special ed program for drug abuse and not doing well in school. When asked, he said his problem was that his parents would not allow him to buy a motorcycle. He admitted that he did not have money to buy one, insure one, take proper driver's education and licensing examinations to own one, even though he had a job. He was asked to figure out how much money he was spending on drugs. Wasting his own money, stealing from his parents and other relatives, and then to figure out, if he saved his own money, did some side jobs for neighbors and family until he was 18, he COULD afford the motorcycle and all it required to legally own one. In fact, he did all, but decided to spend the money on college instead of the motorcycle when he graduated from high school. His priorities had changed as he learned about responsible motorcycle ownership and risk doing the assignments needed for his special ed program. He also gave up drugs, since his stated reason was he could not have a motorcycle, and that was no longer true, he COULD have a motorcycle, just had to buy it himself, not just expect his parents to give it to him.

Printed in the United States
by Baker & Taylor Publisher Services